KANCHIL, the main character in this book, is a popular trickster from Indonesian and Malaysian folklore. Trickster tales in the folklore of most cultures are popular stories about the wise fool, the clown, or the small animal who outwits the larger and more powerful animals. These stories always convey the social values of the culture they come from.

Kanchil is a small deer who lives in the rainforest. Because of his size, he has to live by his wits in order to survive, or else he would be eaten for lunch by the bigger animals of the forest. Kanchil tales are typically a celebration of brains over brawn, of the victory of the less powerful. But like other tricksters, Kanchil sometimes plays tricks on his friends, and sometimes is tricked by other even smaller animals!

For Sierra Gitanjali, whose winsome smile takes her to the finish line every time! — Nathan Kumar Scott

The Great Race
Copyright © Tara Books Pvt. Ltd. 2011

For the text:
Nathan Kumar Scott

For the illustrations:
Jagdish Chitara

For this edition:
Tara Books, India, tarabooks.com and
Tara Publishing Ltd., UK, tarabooks.com/uk

Design: Nia Murphy
Production: C. Arumugam
Photographs: Jonathan Yamakami
Printed in China through Asia Pacific Offset

ISBN: 978-93-80340-15-9

THE GREAT RACE

An Indonesian Trickster Tale

Retold by

Nathan Kumar Scott

Art by

Jagdish Chitara

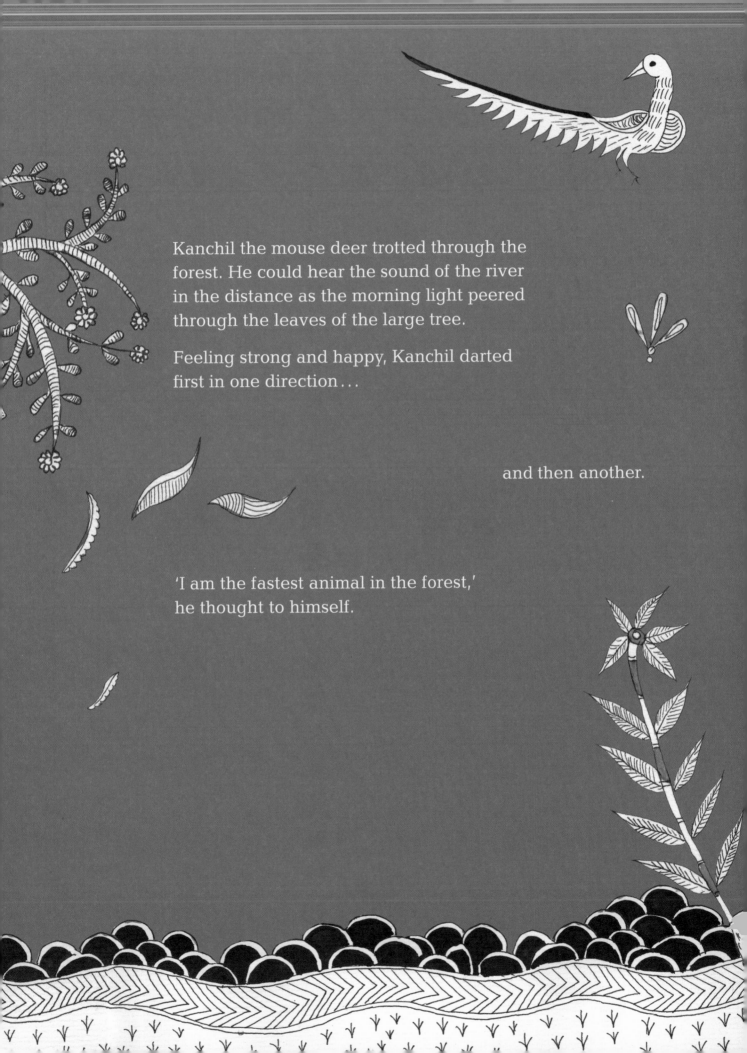

Kanchil the mouse deer trotted through the
forest. He could hear the sound of the river
in the distance as the morning light peered
through the leaves of the large tree.

Feeling strong and happy, Kanchil darted
first in one direction...

and then another.

'I am the fastest animal in the forest,'
he thought to himself.

Yes, Kanchil was much faster on his feet than
his friend Gajah the elephant...

or Babi the wild boar.

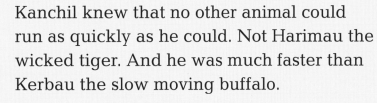

Kanchil knew that no other animal could run as quickly as he could. Not Harimau the wicked tiger. And he was much faster than Kerbau the slow moving buffalo.

Although Buwaya the crocodile had fast moving jaws, Kanchil had escaped from her many times.

Suddenly Kanchil thought of an idea! He would challenge the other animals to a race. It would be

THE GREAT RACE OF THE JUNGLE.

Still thinking about The Great Race, Kanchil
came to the mighty river that flowed through
the forest. He saw several animals gathered
there to drink the cool water and wanted to
share his plan with them.

'Guess what?' Kanchil called as he approached.
'I have an idea. I think we should have a race.
A race to see who is the fastest animal in the
forest.'

'A race?' said Gajah, 'What a good idea!'

'I challenge any animal in this forest to beat me in a race,' Kanchil announced.

Just then Kakatua, the scarlet macaw flew down onto a nearby branch.

'Kakatua, will you please let the whole jungle know that I challenge any animal to a race? We will see who is the fastest animal in the forest.'

'Kaaa
kaaa

a race

a RACE,'

cried Kakatua.

'Kanchil challenges any animal to a race.'
And with that, she took off flying low through
the forest.

'A race, A RACE. Come see The Great Race.

Kaaa,

KAAA.'

Before long, every animal in the forest
had heard about The Great Race. Kanchil
then appeared, skipping happily down the
riverbank.

'Who is going to race me?' he asked.
'Are you, Gajah? Or you, Harimau? Think twice,
because I am the fastest animal in the forest.'

No one spoke a word. Kanchil looked around
at the animals who were gathered. 'Will no one
race me? Not one of you?'

Then Kanchil heard a tiny voice.

'I will,' it said.

'Who said that?' asked Kanchil
turning around quickly.

'I did,' said the tiny voice.
'I will beat you at your race.'

'Who are you?' said Kanchil.
'And where are you?'

'I am Pelan. Pelan the snail.
Look down.'

Kanchil looked down and then laughed.
'YOU? You will race me? Who ever heard
of a snail racing a deer?'

Laughter rippled out through the
gathered animals.

Then in a loud voice Kanchil announced,
'If nobody else will race me, I will race Pelan
the snail. We will race from the big tree here by
the river, along the riverbank, all the way down to
the waterfall. Whoever gets there first will be
the winner.'

Harimau the tiger stepped forward.
'I will be the referee. Gajah, you go down to
the waterfall and wait at the finish line.'

Kanchil and Pelan took their places, while
Gajah disappeared toward the finish line.

Then, in a booming voice, Harimau counted,

'Three...

two...

one...

GO!'

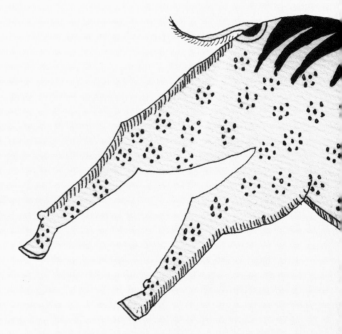

The race began!

Kanchil took off quickly, but soon stopped to rest and eat some grass. He was not worried. There was no way Pelan the snail would beat him.

He went down to the river to get a long drink, and then continued happily on towards the waterfall.

The animals were all paying attention to Kanchil. No one was looking at Pelan.

At the waterfall Gajah had drawn a line in the sand beside the riverbank. When Kanchil finally arrived, who do you think was already there?

'Pelan?! How did you get here so quickly?'

All the animals were amazed!
Had Pelan beaten Kanchil?

Gajah stood on a rock near the waterfall.
'Pelan is the winner!'

Kanchil was shocked. How could a
snail have possibly beaten him? Did
Pelan ride on a branch down the river?

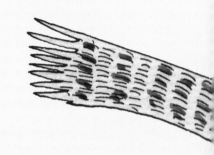

Kanchil had to find a way to beat Pelan.
Thinking quickly, he challenged Pelan to a
new race. This time from the waterfall back
up to the big tree against the flow of the river,
so Pelan could not get a free ride.

Once again, the racers took their places,
while Gajah returned to the finish line at the
big tree and Harimau counted.

GO!'

one...

two...

'Three...

They were off, and this time Kanchil didn't stop along the way. He ran as fast as his little legs would carry him. He raced up along the river, he saw the big tree, he saw Gajah up ahead of him waiting at the finish line, and then he saw…

PELAN!

How could Pelan have beaten him again?
And yet, there he was, the same little snail
with his shell on his back, barely out of
breath.

The Great Race was over. Pelan the snail
had won! Not once but twice.

Kanchil had been beaten, fair and square.
Yet nobody quite knew how.

How did a slow snail beat a fast deer?

Nobody noticed Pelan smile...

at his twin brother.

The two snails were happy to have taught Kanchil a lesson!

Painters of the Cloth of the Mother Goddess

Jagdish Chitara, the artist who painted the illustrations for this book, belongs to a traditional group of artisans known as Waghari. The Waghari people are a particularly poor and marginalised community. Originally nomads, they would roam around the banks of the Sabarmati river in Gujarat, creating a special ritual cloth for the Mother Goddess, worshipped by poor people considered low in the caste system. Called Mata Ni Pachedi – literally the Cloth of the Mother – this fabric was washed in the river waters, block printed and painted, then painstakingly dyed with natural pigments. The beautiful swathes of cloth were used not only as offerings, but also draped to form a temporary shrine for the Goddess.

Although the Waghari's way of life has changed today – many of them, like Jagdish, now live in towns and cities – they still create the traditional sacred cloth, in the old way. The colours are always blood red, black and white. The figure of the Mother Goddess, depicting the myths and stories around her, is central. She is within a grid evoking the architecture of temple doors and alcoves, and around her are attendent gods and their animal companions, with their own narratives.

The ritual function of the Mata Ni Pachedi continues to exist for the so-called lower caste communities. But these beautiful textiles are also part of a growing art market that caters to upper caste and middle class clients, who use them to decorate their homes. While traditional painters earn